MOONBEAMS

written by Marcia Trimble

illustrated by Sid Bingham

FOR SANTA

Published by Images Press

Publisher's Cataloging-in-Publication
(Provided by Quality Books, Inc.)

Trimble, Marcia.
Moonbeams for Santa / by Marcia Trimble ;
illustrated by Sid Bingham. -- 1st ed.
p. cm.
ISBN: 1-891577-89-1
LCCN: 00-93654
SUMMARY: Gibbous' spirits are mighty low until he discovers his inner glow and reveres his role in lighting the way for Santa. He shines over the tops of many a chimney and proudly wears the shadow that is his identity.
Audience: Ages 4-9

1. Moon--Phases--Juvenile fiction. 2. Christmas--Juvenile fiction. [1. Moon--Phases--fiction. 2. Christmas--fiction.]
I. Bingham, Sid II. Title.

PZ7.T7352Mo 2001 [E]
QBI01-700016

10 9 8 7 6 5 4 3 2 1

Text set in Myriad Tilt, Postino Italic, and Sand.
Book design by MontiGraphics.

Printed in Hong Kong by South China Printing Co. (1988) Ltd.
on totally chlorine-free Nymolla Matte Art paper.

To Malinda,

for showing me that
moonlight can be many things...
an inner glow,
a light for your journey,
a shared experience, a gift,
a show-off...
but most of all,
a Gibbous moonscape
that won't go unnoticed.

- M.T.

To Patty

- S.B.

Santa was
old-fashioned.

Santa wanted
old-fashioned
moonlight
for his
old-fashioned
Christmas flight.

He had to know
if
his moon friend
was ready to glow.

As Santa
was steering
his sleigh
into the moonstop,
he called,

"Old Gibbous Moonface, HO! HO! HO!
What's the moonlight forecast
for a Santa on-the-go?

Will you be shining for my flight?

Will you please wait until I get home
before you turn out your light?

And...HO! HO! HO!
Do you have a Christmas wish,
Gibbous?"

Gibbous
grumbled back,

*"I'm just
a humpy
bumpy moon
sittin'
in the sky,
stuck with
this shadow
I wear.*

*I need
more glow.*

*I need
more flair."*

top
E
MOON SPECIALS
DRINKS SODAS
SPECIALS 2 EGGS
MOON ROCK
MOON SHAKES
MOON MENU

"Earthlings don't
ooh and aah
over
my slumpy
shape.

Their eyes
look up
but never linger
on
my moonscape.

Look at me...
more than half
but less
than full...
waxing
'n waning,
waxing
'n waning."

***"You can't
sit around
complaining,
Ol' Moon Friend,"***

said Santa.

***"Better tell me
your wish."***

"Oh, Santa," said Gibbous,
"I wish I could hide
my lopsided side.

A round moonface is the style,
year after year.
FULL MOON shines from ear to ear.

I want to change these phases of mine.
That's it. That's my wish.
I want more shine.
So what do you say, Santa?
Will you polish my shadow?"

"What!

Shrink your shadow?"

said Santa.

"Ho! Ho! Ho!
More shine
will phase you
right out
as you orbit
the earth...
WITHOUT
A DOUBT!

Your
humpy bumpy
shape
is Y-O-U,"

Gibbous heard
Santa shout.

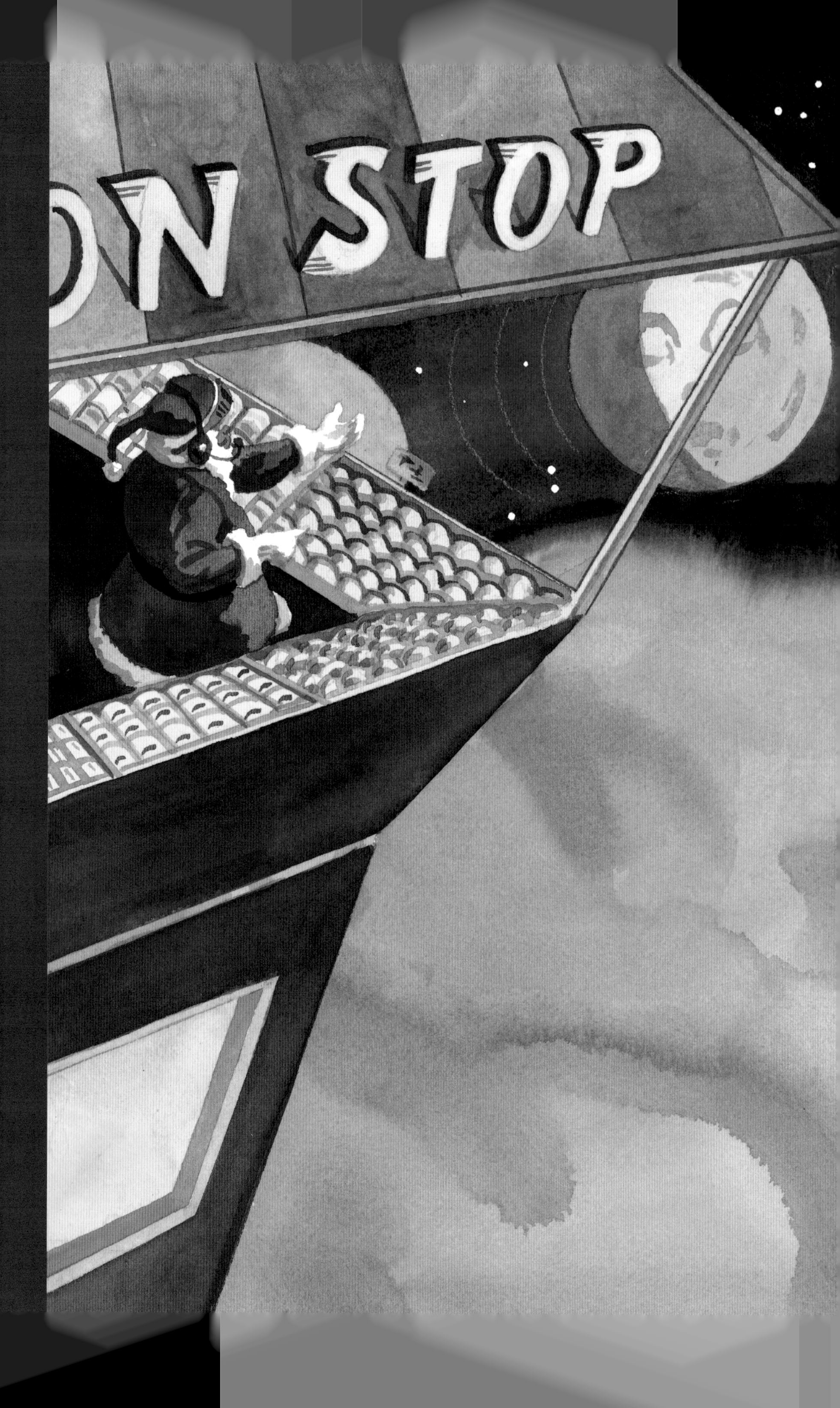

"Polishing your shadow
would make FULL MOON grin.
I wouldn't be able to stop him
from phasing right in."

"Listen,
humpy bumpy
Gibbous...
As you travel
'round
the earth
you play
a double role.

Without
YOUR phases
I couldn't meet
my goal.

I depend on you
to shine down
the chimney
tops
of all
the houses
where I deliver
presents
to kids, Moms,
and Pops.

And
I expect you
to WANE...
in time
to guide
me home
to Candy Cane
Lane.

I'm not counting on
FULL
or QUARTER
or CRESCENT
or NEW.

The moonface
I'm counting on, GIBBOUS,
is YOU!"

"You should know
how much
your shine
is worth,
Ol' Moon Friend,
as you tag along
with Earth,
lighting places
with your team
of eight
moonfaces.

FULL MOON
gets
ONE turn
to shine.
But you get
TWO.

So...HO! HO! HO! Gibbous,
Why so blue?"

Thinking about
finding a gift
for Gibbous
was filling Santa
with pleasure...
like digging
for treasure.

But first
he must unearth
a bucket of mirth...
to pour
on a moonful
of tears...
his biggest
challenge
in years and years.

So Santa opened
the moonchest
and rummaged
around
in its electrical
nest.

As the chest
turned its gears,
tubas oompah'd
in his ears.

It was the Holiday Parade
marching down 5th Avenue.

Crowds were lined up
along with a TV camera crew.

Could it be a dream
that THE MOON ON PARADE
was this year's holiday theme?

"Ho! Ho! Ho!
Gibbous,
it's a parade.

The phases
of the moon
are displayed
by kids
in costume.

The kids
are rolling
along,
side by side...
like a moon
moving along
on
its monthly
ride.

FULL MOON skates by
the crowd
just ONCE...
but Gibbous skates by
TWICE...
to be precise."

"Now
FULL MOON
is bowing,
almost
to his toe.
The crowd
is cheering
as
he shows off
his glow.

But wait!"
said Santa.

"FULL MOON's
moment
of glory
dims.

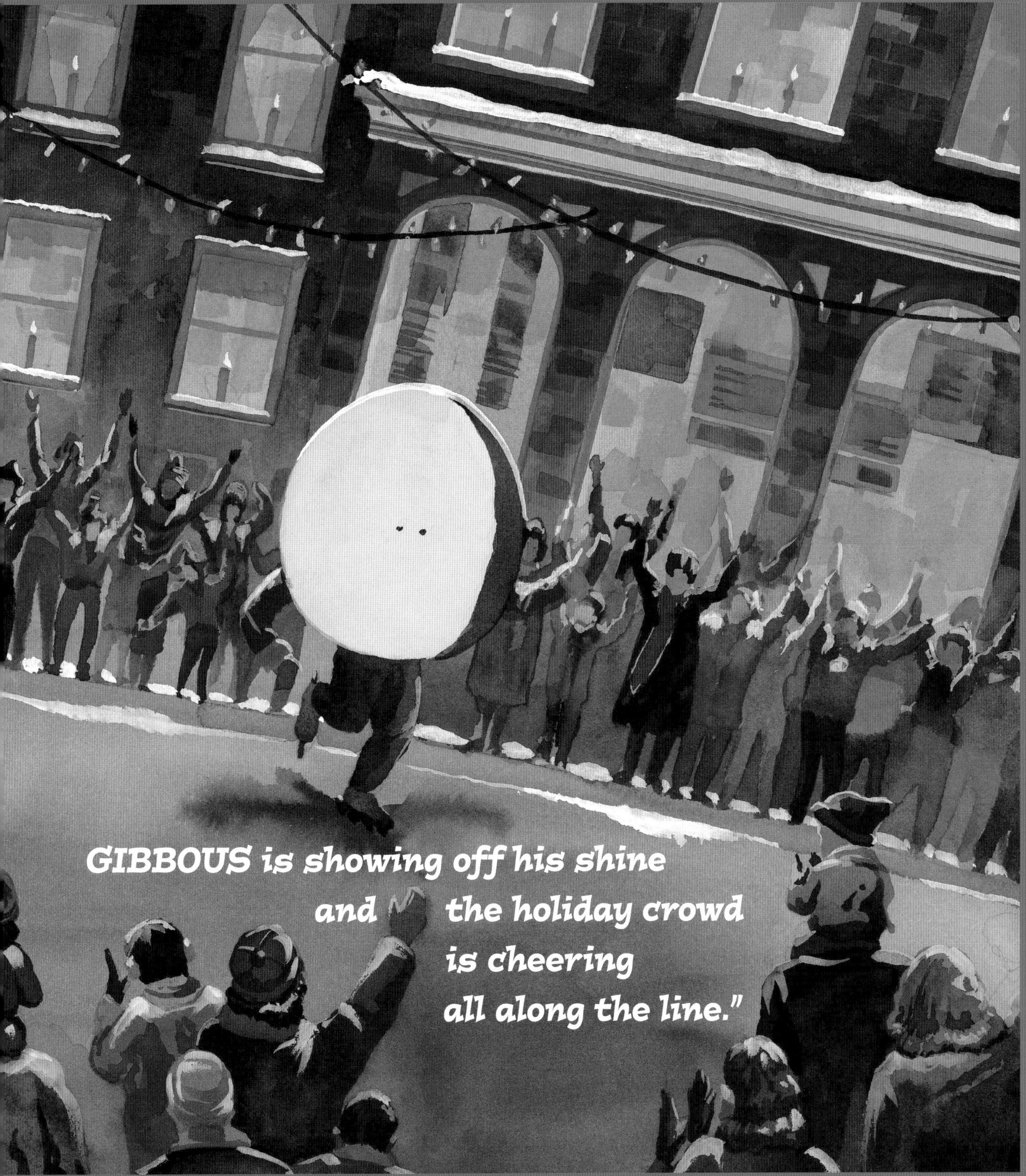

GIBBOUS is showing off his shine
and the holiday crowd
is cheering
all along the line."

"But...what is
that voice
booming out
in the crowd,
booming
so loud...
shouting
Ho! Ho! Ho!
above all
the applause?

Well!
It's the voice
of a Dad,
pretending
he's Santa Claus.

He's rented
a costume
and
belted it tight
after
he stuffed in
three pillows
to get the look
right.

The two Gibbous kids,
who shine equally,
are the stars of this Dad's family tree.

The crowd loves those two kids
rolling together below
because they love YOU, Gibbous,

Ho! Ho! Ho!"

As soon as
all of the cheers
had dried
Gibbous's tears,
Santa's sleigh
floated away,
but Santa called
from afar.

***"Will you
light my way,
Gibbous?
Will you help me
along
on my flight?"***

Gibbous wished
and wished
with all of his light.

*"I wish I may.
I wish I might...
grant the wish
you wish
tonight."*

And his wish,
sparkling
like a firefly,
turned into
a moonbyte*
flashing
across the sky.

Gibbous had waxed
almost to the max
when a light flashed back
across the sky...
like a shooting star,
a thank you from Santa:
a light from the brightest quasar.

Gibbous's wish for more shine
was about to come true
as the quasar's light
struck his moongate
and flashed right on
through.

kwa'sar:
a heavenly object
that emits radio waves
and a powerful blue light

And now
with his glow
hidden inside,
warming his toes,
Gibbous glistened
like a shower
of moonbows.

And
Santa called
one more time,
from afar,

***"GIBBOUS,
listen,
from wherever
you are.***

***Thanks to you,
I'll be swinging
my pack
like a tether
and I'll fly
as light as
a feather
when I wave...***

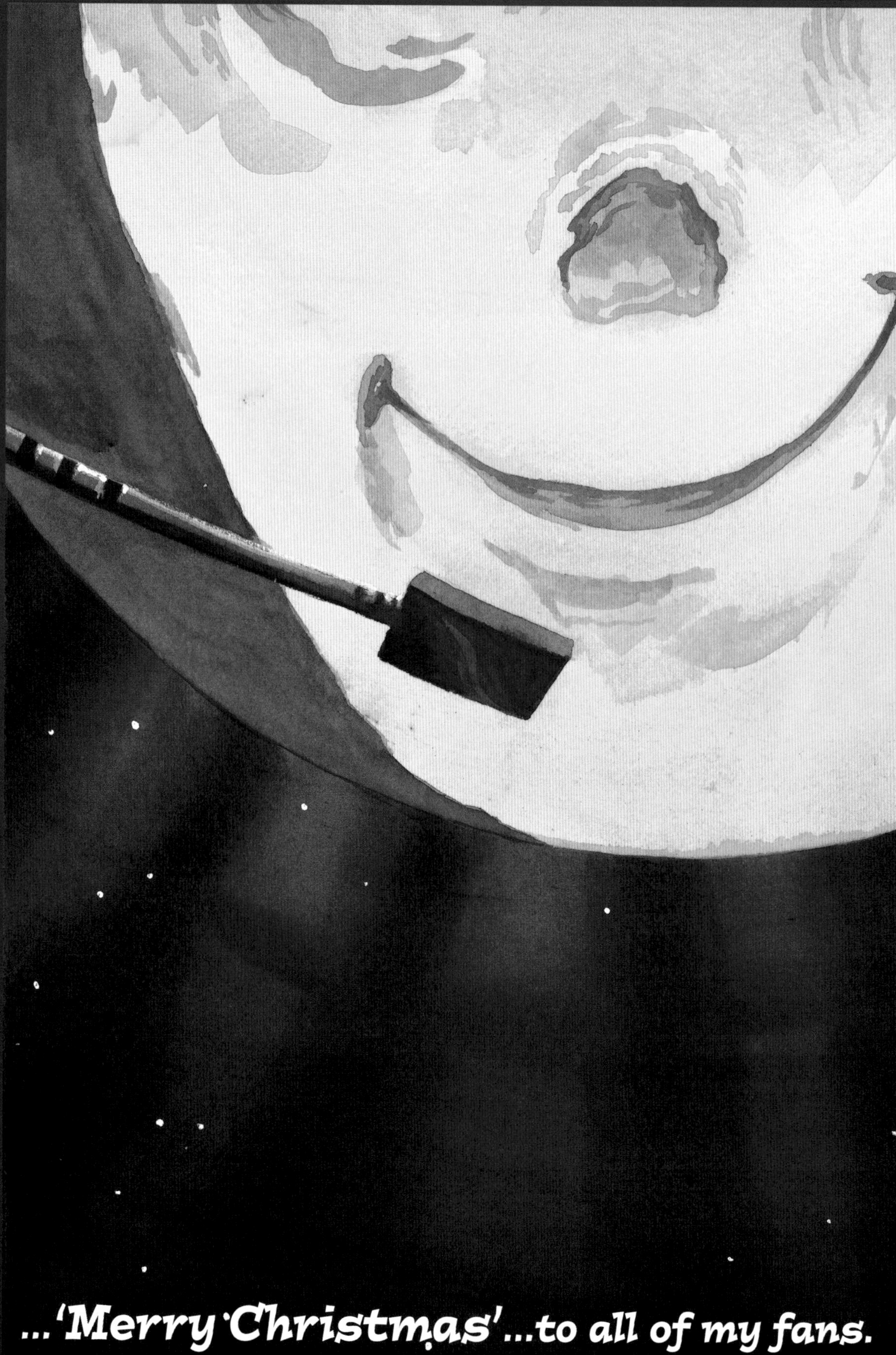

***...'Merry Christmas'...to all of my fans.
Time flies...on with the plans!"***

Please hold reservations...each year
for Santa and Rudolph
and the eight other reindeer.
Will confirm next December via satellite.
Merry moonbeams to all...
and to all a moon night.

Gibbous wished
that FULL MOON
would get on
with his reign
so he could
wear his shadow...
to wane.

Santa would
be waiting
at the moonstop,
as planned,
picking out
a souvenir
for Mrs. Claus
at the
Moonlighting Stand.

Gibbous gleamed
one more gleam
before waxing
from sight,
flashing
the last bit
of glow
with his own
inner light.

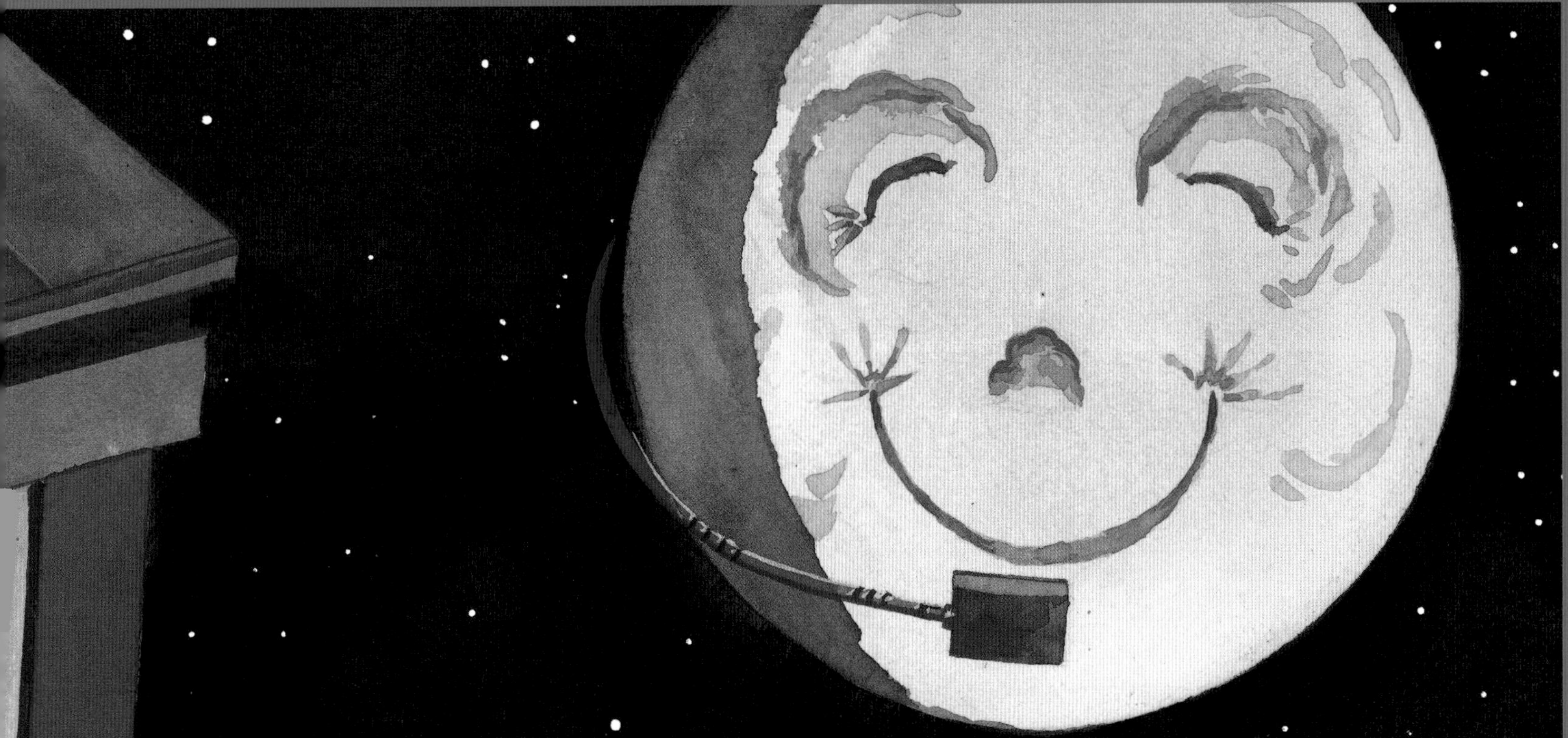

"I'm not a humpy bumpy moon that complains.
I'm the brightest moon that waxes AND wanes.
Because I'm so good in my double role...
Santa counts on ME
to help meet his goal.
I could be a show-off with all of my flair
but with moonbeams inside
I don't need earthlings to stare.

Best of all,
I now know
that the light
beamed from Santa
fired up the moon shine
that was already mine...
but was hiding in there."

From now on,
Gibbous
would stick
with his shadow
and take turns
with his team.

He had gotten
more
than he'd wished
for...
his own
inner glow
AND
TWO turns
to beam.

Every year
Gibbous
would shine
for
Santa's encore.

And earthlings could send wishes to Santa,

forevermore.

Until the moons of December...
Santa, take care.

With flair, Gibbous

P. S. Delivery for Mrs. Claus...
one Gibbous moonbeam.

Man on the Moon

Neil Armstrong, a United States astronaut, was the first person to set foot on the moon. On July 20, 1969, he and Edwin E. Aldrin, Jr., landed the Apollo 11 lunar module on the moon, left the module, explored the lunar surface, and returned to earth with typical dark gray moon rocks. Stories about a moon made of green cheese are truly fairy tales!

Why the Moon Has Phases

The moon changes from new moon to full moon and back again every 29 1/2 days. The phases are caused by the moon's orbit around the earth as the earth and moon travel around the sun. Half of the moon is always in sunlight, but varying amounts of the lighted side are visible from the earth, so the moon seems to change shape from day to day as it goes through phases.

Full Moon
Waxing Gibbous
First Quarter
Waxing Crescent
New Moon
Waning Crescent
Last Quarter
Waning Gibbous
MOON

Credits: World Book Encyclopedia